Little Purple Hen

by Liza Charlesworth

ISBN: 978-1-338-89040-2

Designer: Cynthia Ng; Illustrated by John Lund

1 2 3 4 5 6 7 8 9 10   68   31 30 29 28 27 26 25 24 23 22

Printed in Jiaxing, China. First printing, January 2023.

This is Little Purple Hen.
She lives in a big red barn.
Little Purple Hen never ever likes
to get a bit of help.
"I can do it all by myself!" she exclaims.

One day, Little Purple Hen has a BIG idea.
"Let's have a barn party!" she says to
her pals, Pig, Cow, Sheep, and Dog.
"*OINK, MOO, BAAH, RUFF*!
Sounds grand!" they respond.

"Yippee!" says Little Purple Hen.
"Time to make the invitations."
"Can I help you?" asks her pal, Pig.
"NOPE!" says Little Purple Hen.
"I can do it all by myself."

Little Purple Hen gets right to work.
Write, write, draw, draw.
The invitations look awesome!
Making them is hard,
so Little Purple Hen feels a bit tired.

5

But Little Purple Hen is NOT done yet.
"Time to make cupcakes," she says.
"Can I help you?" asks her pal, Cow.
"NOPE!" says Little Purple Hen.
"I can do it all by myself."

Little Purple Hen gets right to work.
Mix, mix, bake, bake.
The cupcakes look awesome!
Making them is hard,
so Purple Hen feels more tired.

But Little Purple Hen is NOT done yet.
"Time to clean up the barn," she says.
"Can I help you?" asks her pal, Sheep.
"NOPE!" says Little Purple Hen.
"I can do it all by myself."

Little Purple Hen gets right to work.
Dust, dust, sweep, sweep.
The barn looks awesome!
Cleaning it up is hard,
so Little Purple Hen feels VERY tired.

But Little Purple Hen is NOT done yet.
"Time to decorate the barn," she says.
"Can I help you?" asks her pal, Dog.
"NOPE!" says Little Purple Hen.
"I can do it all by myself."

Little Purple Hen begins to blow up balloons.
"I am SOOOOO tired," she says.
"I will lay down and rest for just a minute."
But before long...
ZZZZZZZZZZZZZZZZZZZZZZZZZZ!

Little Purple Hen takes a good long nap.
Sleep, sleep, sleep, sleep.
Then… *"OINK, MOO, BAAH, RUFF!"*
Her friends come over and wake her up.
"It's 7:00! Time for the party!" they shout.

UH-OH! Little Purple Hen is upset.
"I am SOOOOO sorry!" she cries.
"I wanted to do everything all by myself
and now the party is NOT ready."

"Don't cry," say her kind pals.
"Just relax. We're happy to help!"
So Pig blows up the rest of the balloons.
And Cow hangs them all around.
And Sheep puts out the cupcakes.
And Dog gets the music set up.

Soon, the barn is ready for the party.
And Little Purple Hen has learned a BIG lesson.
"From now on, I will always ask for help
when I need it," she says.
"*OINK, MOO, BAAH, RUFF!*
That's a great plan!" respond her pals.

Then, Dog puts on some awesome tunes.
"Time for everyone to get on the dance floor!"
shouts Little Purple Hen with glee.
And they do....
Hip, hop, boogie-oogie!